I Know Someone with
Asthma

Vic Parker

Heinemann Library
Chicago, Illinois

www.heinemannraintree.com
Visit our website to find out
more information about
Heinemann-Raintree books.

To order:

☎ Phone 888-454-2279

💻 Visit www.heinemannraintree.com
to browse our catalog and order online.

Edited by Rebecca Rissman, Daniel Nunn,
  and Siân Smith
Designed by Joanna Hinton Malivoire
Picture research by Mica Brancic
Originated by Capstone Global Library
Printed in the United States of America by
Worzalla Publishing

14 13 12 11 10
10 9 8 7 6 5 4 3 2 1

Library of Congress Cataloging-in-Publication Data
Parker, Victoria.
  I know someone with asthma / Vic Parker.
    p. cm.—(Understanding health issues)
  Includes bibliographical references and index.
  ISBN 978-1-4329-4556-5 (hc)
  ISBN 978-1-4329-4572-5 (pb)
  1. Asthma—Juvenile literature. I. Title.
  RC591.P365 2011
  616.2'38—dc22   2010026417

Acknowledgments
We would like to thank the following for permission
to reproduce photographs: AP/Press Association
Photos p. 20 (LM Otero); Corbis pp. 14 (© JLP/Jose L.
Pelaez), 24 (Icon SMI/© Dustin Snipes); Getty Images
pp. 10 (Michael Zagaris), 22 (Science Photo Library/
Ian Hooton), 25 (Getty Images for British Gas);
iStockphoto.com pp. 5 (© Marilyn Nieves), 9 (© George
M Muresan), 17 (© RMAX), 18 (© Chad Thomas);
Photolibrary p. 16 (Creatas); Science Photo Library pp.
4 (J. Lama, Publiphoto Diffusion), 7 (Peter Gardiner),
13 (Coneyl Jay), 21 (RVI, Newcastle-Upon-Tyne/
Simon Fraser); Shutterstock pp. 11 (© Paul Prescott),
12 (Monkey Business Images), 19 (© Ken Inness), 26
(Jeanne Hatch), 27 (Monkey Business Images (Mandy
Godbehear).

Cover photograph of a girl using an inhaler to treat an
asthma attack reproduced with permission of Science
Photo Library (Ian Hooton).

We would like to thank Matthew Siegel and Ashley
Wolinski for their invaluable help in the preparation of
this book.

Every effort has been made to contact copyright
holders of any material reproduced in this book. Any
omissions will be rectified in subsequent printings if
notice is given to the publisher.

All the Internet addresses (URLs) given in this book
were valid at the time of going to press. However, due
to the dynamic nature of the Internet, some addresses
may have changed, or sites may have changed or
ceased to exist since publication. While the author and
publisher regret any inconvenience this may cause
readers, no responsibility for any such changes can be
accepted by either the author or the publisher.

Contents

Some words are printed in bold, **like this**. You can
find out what they mean in the glossary.

Do You Know Someone with Asthma?

You might have a friend with asthma. Asthma is a **medical condition** that affects parts of the chest. People with asthma have problems with their breathing.

People with asthma may cough a lot, even when they are well.

People with asthma can be more likely to wheeze when exercising outdoors than when exercising indoors.

You might be able to tell that people have asthma by listening to their breathing. They may often **wheeze**. They may get out of breath quickly when they exercise.

What Is Asthma?

When we breathe in, we take in air through our nose and mouth. The air goes down into our lungs through tubes called **airways**.

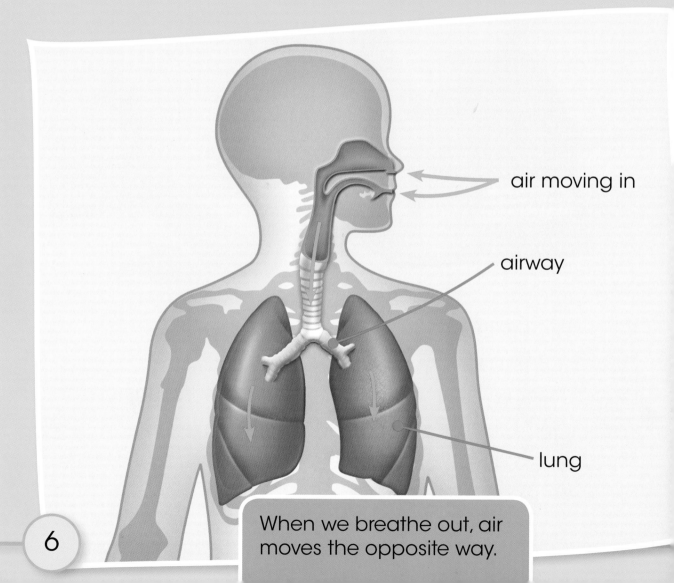

air moving in

airway

lung

When we breathe out, air moves the opposite way.

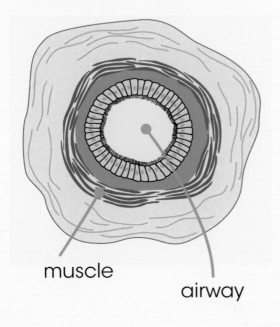

inside a normal airway

muscle

airway

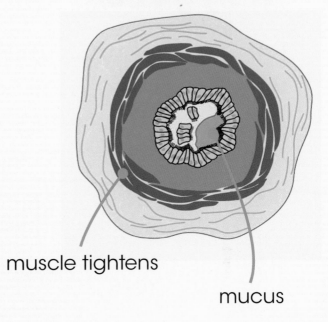

an airway during
an asthma attack

muscle tightens

mucus

When people have asthma, sometimes the insides of their airways become swollen and makes gooey stuff called mucus. The muscles around the airways also get tighter. This blocks the airways, making it hard to breathe. This is called an **asthma attack**.

Asthma Attacks and Triggers

People can have **asthma attacks** when they are around what doctors call "**triggers**." A trigger is something that can cause an asthma attack or make an attack worse.

Triggers can include:

- cold air
- dust
- furry and feathery animals
- molds
- some foods
- exercise
- strong smells
- pollution in the air
- strong emotions such as stress.

For some people, cold air is an asthma trigger.

One person's asthma triggers can be different from another's. A person's asthma triggers can also change from time to time.

Everyone Is Different

Some people need more help with asthma than others.

Some people with asthma find that they are short of breath a lot of the time. They might get **asthma attacks** quite often.

Other people with asthma go for a long time without being affected very much. Then a **trigger** can cause an asthma attack.

When people know they will be around things that trigger their asthma, such as feathers, they can take medicine to help control it.

Who Gets Asthma?

Anyone can get asthma, at any time. However, it can run in families, and people often develop it as children or teenagers. Once you have asthma, you usually have it for life.

It is not possible to catch asthma from someone else.

Tests for asthma include blowing as hard as you can into a spirometer or a peak flow machine. These machines show how well air passes through your **airways**.

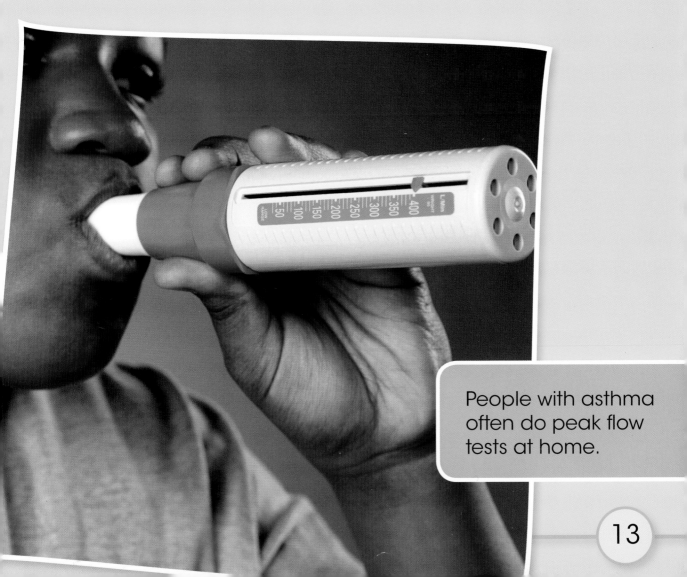

People with asthma often do peak flow tests at home.

Living with Asthma

There is currently no **cure** for asthma. However, someone with asthma can lead a full, fun life. It is helpful to keep a diary of **triggers** and **symptoms** or signs of asthma, to discuss with a doctor.

People with asthma can work with their doctors to keep it under control.

People can plan how to avoid their triggers. This will keep their symptoms as mild as possible. Some things that might help are shown in the table below.

Trigger	Actions
dust	• Vacuum often. • Dust often, with a damp duster. • Wash soft toys often.
animals	• Ideally, have no pets. • If you have pets, wash them often and do not let them in your bedroom.
cold air	• Try to play indoors and do indoor sports on cold days.
pollen	• Don't play outside when the **pollen count** is high.

Medicines to Control Asthma

In addition to avoiding **triggers**, many people with asthma need to take medicine every day. This is to control the swelling in their **airways** and stop it from getting worse.

If people can control their asthma, they can do any sport that someone without asthma can do.

People with asthma each need to use their own inhaler.

This type of medicine is called controller medicine. Some controller medicines are swallowed as tablets or liquids. But many are breathed in through **inhalers**.

Treatments to Relieve Asthma

If people with asthma feel their **symptoms** are getting worse, they can take reliever medicine. This relaxes the muscles around their **airways** and usually works very quickly.

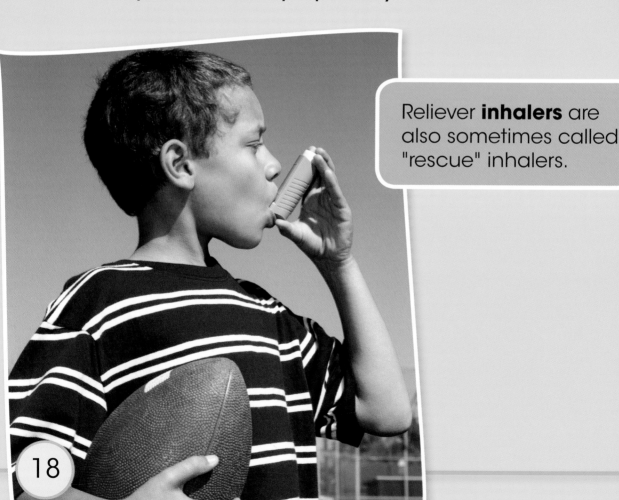

Reliever **inhalers** are also sometimes called "rescue" inhalers.

Reliever medicine can also help people with asthma to exercise. If they take it just before exercising, it will keep their airways open. Then they can enjoy their sport.

People with asthma can still become excellent athletes.

Emergency!

Occasionally, when someone is having an **asthma attack**, taking reliever medicine may not stop the attack from getting worse. Then the person needs to go to the hospital right away.

It is a good idea to call an ambulance if someone needs urgent medical help.

At the hospital, doctors and nurses can give stronger medicines to someone having a severe asthma attack. This usually helps them feel much better.

This equipment can help someone having a severe asthma attack to breathe in strong medicine.

How Can You Help Someone Having an Asthma Attack?

If a friend has a sudden **asthma attack**, it is important to stay calm. Your friend should use a reliever **inhaler** right away. You should get help from an adult.

A person having an asthma attack needs to stay calm and try to relax.

How you can help:
- You can get your friend his or her reliever inhaler.
- Tell an adult right away.
- Help your friend to stay calm by keeping calm, too.
- Encourage your friend to sit down instead of lying down or standing up.

Some people can have asthma attacks that are caused by certain foods, such as eggs. These people should always carry a special **injection** with them that can stop the attack for a while.

Famous People

David Beckham has had asthma since he was a child. This has not stopped him from becoming a successful soccer player.

David Beckham is one of the most famous soccer stars in the world.

As part of her training, Rebecca Adlington has to run and do gym workouts, in addition to swimming.

Chlorine is used in swimming pools to keep water clean. Chlorine can be another asthma **trigger**. But Rebecca Adlington is a British swimmer with asthma who has won two Olympic gold medals!

Being a Good Friend

You can be a good friend to people with asthma by finding out what **triggers** their asthma. Try to do things together that keep you away from their asthma triggers.

Good friends understand each other.

We all have different bodies and personalities.

Living with asthma can be difficult at times. We are all different in many ways. A good friend likes us and values us for who we are.

Asthma: Facts and Fiction

Facts

- Over 34 million Americans have asthma.

- More boys have asthma than girls.

- Colds and the flu can make asthma worse.

Fiction

(?) People with asthma are short of breath all the time.

WRONG! Some have **symptoms** only occasionally.

(?) People with asthma can't exercise.

WRONG! Someone with controlled asthma can get lots of exercise.

(?) You aren't more likely to get asthma if your parents smoke.

WRONG! Children whose parents smoke are 1½ times more likely to develop asthma.

Glossary

airway tube in your body that air travels through to get to your lungs

asthma attack when someone has difficulty breathing due to asthma

cure medical treatment that makes someone better

inhaler small piece of equipment you use to breathe in certain medicines

injection needle that puts medicine into a person's body

medical condition health problem that a person has for a long time or for life

pollen count measurement of the amount of pollen in the air. Pollen is made by plants.

symptoms signs of an illness

trigger something that can cause an asthma attack or make an attack worse

wheeze make a high, rough noise due to difficulties breathing

Find Out More

Books to Read

Bee, Peta. *I Have Asthma (Taking Care of Myself)*. New York: Gareth Stevens: 2011.

Powell, Jillian. *Asthma (Feeling Sick)*. Mankato, Minn.: Cherrytree, 2007.

Robbins, Lynette. *How to Deal with Asthma (Kids' Health)*. New York: PowerKids, 2010.

Websites

http://kidshealth.org/kid/centers/asthma_center.html
Visit Kids' Health to watch an animation that shows what happens during an asthma attack.

www.aafa.org
Learn more about dealing with asthma at this website of the Asthma and Allergy Foundation of America.

Index